# Dear Parent:
## Your child's love of reading starts here!

Every child learns to read in a different way and at his or her own speed. You can help your young reader improve and become more confident by encouraging his or her own interests and abilities. You can also guide your child's spiritual development by reading stories with biblical values and Bible stories, like I Can Read! books published by Zonderkidz. From books your child reads with you to the first books he or she reads alone, there are I Can Read! books for every stage of reading:

**SHARED READING**
Basic language, word repetition, and whimsical illustrations, ideal for sharing with your emergent reader.

**BEGINNING READING**
Short sentences, familiar words, and simple concepts for children eager to read on their own.

**READING WITH HELP**
Engaging stories, longer sentences, and language play for developing readers.

**READING ALONE**
Complex plots, challenging vocabulary, and high-interest topics for the independent reader.

**ADVANCED READING**
Short paragraphs, chapters, and exciting themes for the perfect bridge to chapter books.

**I Can Read!** books have introduced children to the joy of reading since 1957. Featuring award-winning authors and illustrators and a fabulous cast of beloved characters, I Can Read! books set the standard for beginning readers.

A lifetime of discovery begins with the magical words **"I Can Read!"**

*Visit www.icanread.com for information on enriching your child's reading experience.*
*Visit www.zonderkidz.com for more Zonderkidz I Can Read! titles.*

"Share your food with hungry people.
Provide homeless people with a place to stay.'
*Isaiah 58:7*

ZONDERKIDZ

*The Berenstain Bears™ Help the Homeless*
Copyright © 2012 by Berenstain Publishing, Inc.
Illustrations © 2012 by Berenstain Publishing, Inc.

Requests for information should be addressed to:
Zonderkidz, 5300 Patterson Ave SE, Grand Rapids, Michigan 49530

Library of Congress Cataloging-in-Publication Data

Berenstain, Jan, 1923–
    The Berenstain Bears help the homeless / written by Jan and Mike Berenstain.
        p.   cm. — (I can read.)
    Summary: The Bear Scouts fix up an old house for Widow McBear to turn into a
    homeless shelter.
    ISBN 978-0310-72102-4 (softcover)
    [1. Homeless persons—Fiction. 2. Scouting (Youth activity)—Fiction. 3. Bears—Fiction.
    4. Christian life—Fiction.] I. Berenstain, Mike, 1951- II. Title.
    PZ7. B44826Bgr 2012
  [E]—dc22                                                 2010054469

*Editor: Mary Hassinger*
*Art direction & design: Cindy Davis*

*Printed in China*
16 17 /DSC/ 11 10 9 8 7

I Can Read!

BEGINNING READING 1

# The Berenstain Bears.
# Help the
# Homeless

WITHDRAWN

## Story and Pictures By
## Jan and Mike Berenstain

Living Lights™

GOOD DEED SCOUTS

ZONDERVAN.com/
AUTHORTRACKER
follow your favorite authors

The Good Deed Scouts were
trying to think of a good deed to do.
Before they could, Widow McBear
came by.

"Hello, scouts," she said.

"I have a good deed for you."

"That's great!" said Brother.

"What is it?" asked Sister.

"I have an old house on top of
Spook Hill," said Widow McBear.
"No one lives there. It is run down."
"It sounds *spooky*!" said Sister to Lizzy.

"I want to make it a home
for the homeless," said Widow McBear.
"Will you scouts fix it up?"
"Yes, we will!" said the Scouts.

"Here is the key," said Widow McBear.

"You can start tonight."

"Tonight?" said Sister.

The scouts were scared.

Sister thought there might be ghosts.

Brother thought there might be goblins.

Lizzy thought there might be monsters.

But Fred was not scared. It was just
an old house. It would make a
good home for the homeless.
"As the Bible says," Fred pointed out,
"'Rescue the weak and the needy.'"
"Good point, Fred," said Brother.

That night the scouts stood
at the bottom of Spook Hill.

"I am afraid there are ghosts," said Sister.

"I am afraid there are goblins," said Brother.

"I am afraid there are monsters," said Lizzy.

"It is just an empty, old house," said Fred.

"Follow me!"

So up Spook Hill the scouts went.

Sister, Brother, and Lizzy were wrong.

There were no ghosts or goblins

or monsters in the house.

But Fred was wrong too.

The house was not empty.

Lots of eyes were looking out of the

windows. Lots of little eyes—

and one pair of big eyes!

The little eyes belonged to the bats
that lived in the house.

The big eyes belonged to Old Tom.

He was a homeless bear.

He stayed at the spooky, old house.

As the scouts came closer,
Old Tom and the bats
grew afraid.

The scouts walked across the porch.

*Creak! Creak!* went the floor.

Fred turned the doorknob.

*Rattle! Rattle!* went the knob.

Fred pulled the door open.

*Squeeek!* went the door.

Bats came flying out the open door!

*Whoosh!* went the bats.

The scouts went inside.

They saw two big eyes!

"Ghosts!" yelled Sister.

"Goblins!" yelled Brother.

"Monsters!" yelled Lizzy.

"Help!" yelled Old Tom.

"It's Old Tom!" said Brother.

"We see him around town."

"Hello, Tom," said Fred.

"We are the Good Deed Scouts.

We are fixing up this house.

Will you help?"

Old Tom was glad to help.

They started the next day.

They hammered and sawed.

They swept and washed.

They painted and polished.

Soon, the spooky, old house

on top of Spook Hill

looked like new.

29

Widow McBear came to open the new
Spook Hill Homeless Shelter.
She asked Old Tom to stay and take
care of it. All the homeless bears
of Bear Country came to live there.

The bats stayed too.

They lived up in the attic.

"Thank you for helping the homeless, Good Deed Scouts!" said Widow McBear.

"Thank you for giving us a good deed to do," said Brother.

"As the Bible says," Fred pointed out, "'Learn to do right; seek justice. Defend the oppressed.'"

"Good point, Fred!" they all said.